For Darren and Brutus, Derek and Doc—
my grandsons and their adopted manatees

Other books by Jim Arnosky:

Crinkleroot's Book of Animal Tracking
Crinkleroot's Guide to Knowing Butterflies and Moths
Crinkleroot's Guide to Knowing the Birds
Crinkleroot's Guide to Knowing the Trees
Crinkleroot's Guide to Walking in Wild Places
Crinkleroot's Nature Almanac
Crinkleroot's Visit to Crinkle Cove
I Was Born in a Tree and Raised by Bees

SIMON & SCHUSTER BOOKS FOR YOUNG READERS
An imprint of Simon & Schuster Children's Publishing Division
1230 Avenue of the Americas, New York, New York 10020

SAVE THE MANATEE and ADOPT-A-MANATEE are registered trademarks of
Save the Manatee Club, Inc., a nonprofit organization. Used with permission.

Book design by Jennifer Reyes. The text of this book is set in Lomba Medium.
The illustrations are rendered in acrylic and acrylic washes.
Printed in Hong Kong
2 4 6 8 10 9 7 5 3 1
Library of Congress Cataloging-in-Publication Data
Arnosky, Jim.
p.   cm.
Summary: A mother manatee and her baby swim in the warm waters of the Crystal River
in Florida.
ISBN 0-689-81604-9
1. Manatees Juvenile fiction. [1. Manatees Fiction.] I. Title.
PZ10.3.A648Man 2000   [E]—dc21   99-39430   CIP   AC

A Manatee Morning

BY JIM ARNOSKY

Simon & Schuster Books for Young Readers

• *New York   London   Toronto   Sydney   Singapore* •

*I*n the Crystal River,
where the water's warm and clean,
something big is moving.
It's a swimming manatee.

And the things that look like boulders
in the middle of the stream
aren't big old boulders after all.
It's a group of manatees.

Manatees are giants,
as gentle as can be.
They're underwater mammals
that keep surfacing to breathe.

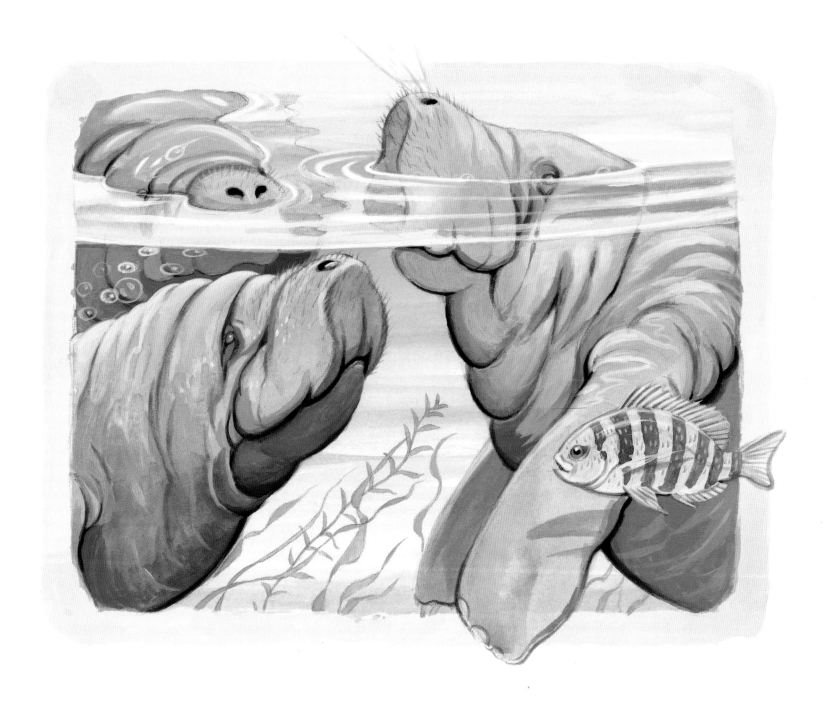

Green water plants
are the only food they need.
When they find their favorite, hyacinth,
they never want to leave.

Look! There's one
much smaller than the others.
It's a baby manatee
swimming with his mother.

See how he follows her
everywhere she goes.
See how she nuzzles him
with her nose.

Manatee baby,
manatee mom,
swimming in the shady pool,
swimming in the sun.

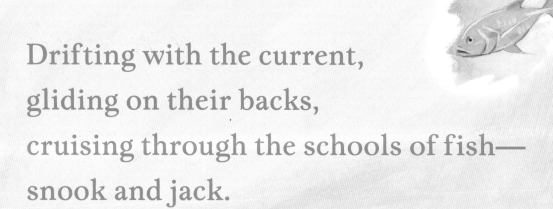

Drifting with the current,
gliding on their backs,
cruising through the schools of fish—
snook and jack.

They swim beneath a pelican
gulping down a bass.
They pass an alligator
sleeping in the grass.

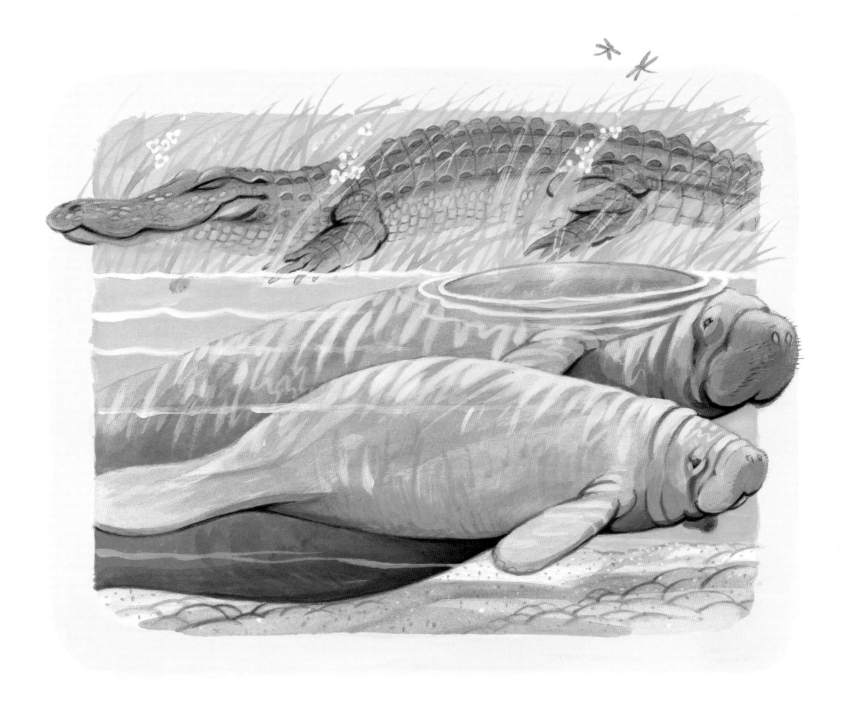

Mother hears a roaring sound
and holds her baby dear
as a motorboat goes churning by,
dangerously near.

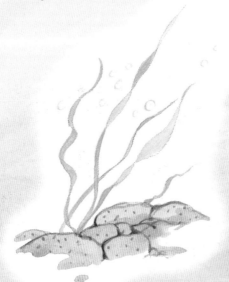

Baby and mom
murmur soft sounds
as sparkling fish surround them
and the water calms down.

In the Crystal River,
where the water's warm and clean,
something big is moving.
It's a swimming manatee.

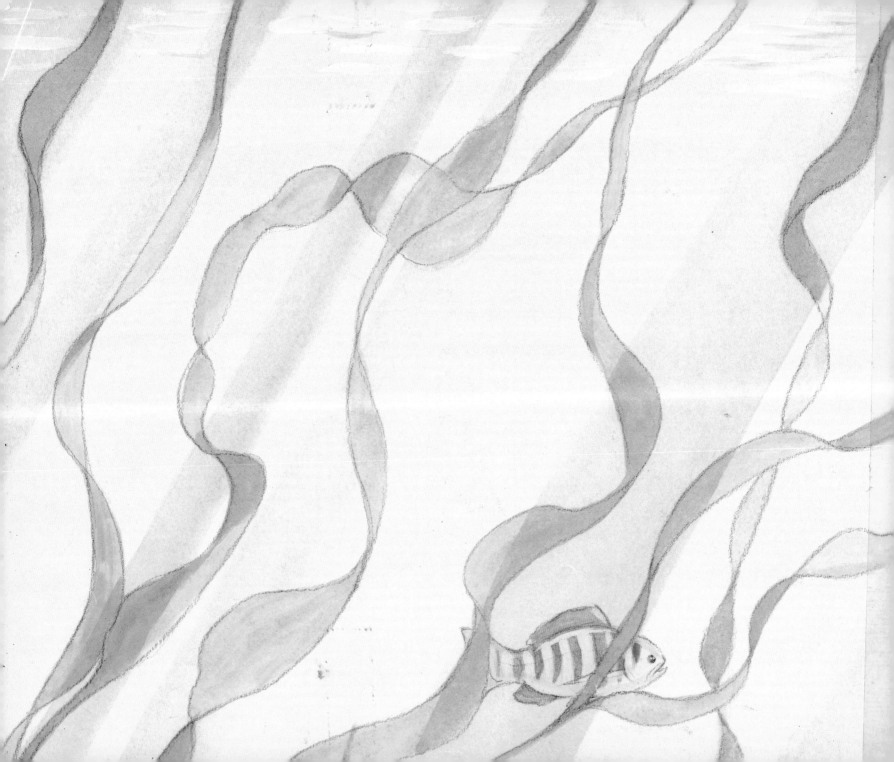